POPPY

and the Mane Mania

*For Donna, who loves singing and hugging
even more than Trolls do*

randomhousekids.com

ISBN 978-1-5247-1705-6 (trade) — ISBN 978-1-5247-1706-3 (lib. bdg.)
ISBN 978-1-5247-1707-0 (ebook)

Printed in the United States of America'

10 9 8 7 6 5 4 3 2 1

POPPY

and the Mane Mania

By David Lewman

Random House 🏠 New York

CHAPTER ONE

Early one bright, sunny morning, Poppy ran through Troll Village toward the Hair in the Air Salon. She didn't want to be late for her appointment with Maddy, the Trolls' expert hairstylist. Poppy's pouf of pink hair had to be absolutely perfect for the big party that night!

As she ran, Poppy sang a happy, bouncy song about getting her hair done. *"This Troll*

1

feels like she's floating on air . . . after Maddy styles her hair! Uh-huh! Yeah, yeah! C'mon! Get it, get it!"

She'd purposely scheduled her appointment with Maddy for first thing in the morning so she'd be the only customer. Poppy loved the peace and quiet of the empty hair salon. She'd close her eyes and listen to the *snip, snip, snip* of Maddy's scissors. Smell the shampoo and hair spray. Feel the comb running through her hair . . .

But it didn't turn out that way.

When Poppy opened the door of the Hair in the Air Salon, the colorful pod was already bustling with customers! Maddy was running from station to station, working on several Trolls' hair at the same time. She somehow managed to go from washing to trimming to drying to brushing without missing a beat.

"Good morning, Poppy!" the Trolls shouted happily.

"Here to get your hair done for the big party?" Cooper asked as Maddy worked on his blue dreadlocks.

"You know it!" Poppy said enthusiastically. She giggled. "Looks like I'm not the only one!"

Maddy paused for a second before she moved to another thick head of hair. "Don't worry, Poppy," she said, touching her arm. "I'll get to you right away!" She looked at all the full chairs. "Well, as soon as a station opens up, anyway."

"No problem," Poppy reassured the busy hairdresser. "I'll just say hello to . . . *Branch*?"

Poppy was surprised to see her friend sitting in a chair with curlers in his blue hair.

"Hi, Poppy," he muttered, shifting in his seat uncomfortably.

She walked over to him. "So you're going to the big party?"

"Yup," Branch said.

"But I thought you didn't like big loud parties," Poppy said.

"That was before we became friends with the Bergens," he explained. "Now I guess parties are pretty safe. As long as they're not *too* loud."

Poppy reached out to touch one of the curlers in Branch's hair. "And you're having your hair done for the party."

Branch drew back from Poppy's hand, a little embarrassed. "Nothing wrong with looking your best, is there?" Secretly, he wanted to look good for Poppy.

"Nothing at all!" Poppy agreed, nodding. She wanted to look good for Branch. "I think it's great that you're getting your hair done. It's just that I don't think I've ever seen you in here before."

"Well, this is my first time," Branch admitted. He leaned forward and whispered, "Am I doing everything right?"

"You're doing everything perfectly!" Poppy said, laughing. "You're sitting still, and you're not squirming. When Maddy works on your hair, do you chat with her?"

Branch looked puzzled. "About what?"

"Oh, anything," Poppy said. "The weather, her family, the party, scrapbooking . . ."

Branch shrugged. "Not really. She's so busy, she just runs over, does something to my hair, and runs off again."

Branch was certainly right about Maddy being super busy. She was moving around the salon constantly, her own swirl of blue hair bobbing with each step. She used a Trimmerbug to snip the ends of Guy Diamond's long silvery hair. To reach the top tips, she had to climb onto a toadstool.

"Remember to sprinkle on plenty of glitter," Guy said in his shimmery voice, which sounded as though he were speaking through a microphone with reverb and other electronic effects.

"Don't worry," Maddy replied. "I will!"

"And if you run out of glitter," said Guy,

shaking off a cloud of the silver stuff, "there's plenty more where that came from!"

But Maddy had already moved on to her next clients. She grabbed a Blowbug and aimed it at Satin and Chenille's damp pink and blue locks. *WHOOOOSH!* The Blowbug blew hot air right at the spot where the twins' hair joined them together.

"Is our hair almost dry?" Satin asked.

"Almost!" Maddy answered, working the Blowbug back and forth.

"Good!" Chenille said. "We have to get back to our dress shop soon!"

"We need plenty of time to finish our outfits for tonight!" Satin explained.

"You will!" Maddy promised. "Don't worry."

Maddy set the Blowbug in a little basket and

picked up a Brusherfly. As she held it over DJ Suki's head, the Brusherfly dragged its long legs through her orange hair. "I think you're going to have to take off your headphones," Maddy told DJ Suki.

"WHAT?" DJ Suki said loudly. "I CAN'T HEAR YOU WITH MY HEADPHONES ON."

Maddy gently lifted one side of the headphones from DJ Suki's ear. "Please take these off so I can get to the hair around your ears."

DJ Suki laughed. "Oh, yeah! That makes total sense!" She took off her headphones and set them down. "How about some tunes? I brought my Wooferbug!"

Next to DJ Suki was her funky Wooferbug. She scratched its back, and it started pumping out a thumpin' dance tune! DJ Suki snapped her fingers. "That's more like it! Yeah! This is my jam! Feel the beat!"

Maddy smiled and nodded. The beat of the music inspired her to move around her salon even faster. She'd have all these Trolls ready for the party in no time!

The first customer to be finished was Cooper. Since he wore a hat all the time, styling his hair was simple. Maddy just had to clean and trim his blue dreadlocks, add a little acorn oil, and . . . voilà! The giraffelike Troll was ready for the celebration!

"Thanks, Maddy!" Cooper said, admiring his reflection in a mirror. "Terrific job, as always! You're the best!"

"Thanks, Cooper!" Maddy said. "Do you

know what you're going to wear to the party?"

Cooper scrunched up his face, thinking. "I'm still not sure. But I'm leaning toward my green hat."

Maddy smiled and nodded. That made sense, since Cooper *always* wore his green hat.

"Here, Poppy," Cooper said, patting the chair he'd been sitting in. "You can take my seat. I'm all done!"

"Thanks!" Poppy said, settling onto the poufy cushion. "You look great!"

"Aw, thanks," Cooper said. He may have even blushed a little, but since his face was already pink, it was hard to tell. With the extra spring in his step, he practically danced out the door.

"I'll get started on you in just a second,

Poppy," Maddy promised. She rushed over to Fuzzbert, who was waiting patiently in a chair. "So—what are we doing today? Trim? New hairdo? Full cut? Perm?"

"UNG GUNG HRM GRN!" Fuzzbert grunted in his own special language, his voice muffled by the long green hair that covered his mouth. In fact, Fuzzbert was *completely* covered in hair, except for his feet and toes.

"Okay," Maddy said a little uncertainly. "How about we start with a wash?"

Making happy little sounds, Fuzzbert nodded with his whole hairy body. Maddy asked him to lean back into the sink, then got to work shampooing his long hair. It took a lot of shampoo, but luckily Maddy had bottles and bottles of it in her closet. When you worked on

Trolls' hair, you went through a lot of shampoo!

While she waited her turn, Poppy reached down into the basket next to her chair and pulled out the latest issue of *Troll Life*. Just as she started to read an article called "Cupcakes: Can You Really Ever Have Too Many?" the front door of the Hair in the Air Salon banged open.

A deep voice shouted, "HELP!"

CHAPTER TWO

The deep voice belonged to Smidge, one of the smallest Trolls around. Though her body was little, her voice was big. And she was strong, too, able to lift heavy weights with her long blue hair. Right now, she looked scared.

Poppy rushed over to her friend. "What's the matter, Smidge?"

"It's Karma!" Smidge told Poppy in an even

deeper voice than usual. "She's missing!"

"Missing?" Poppy asked. "What do you mean? Since when?"

Everyone in the salon was quiet, listening to Smidge. DJ Suki tapped her Wooferbug, signaling the critter to stop playing music. You could hear a pin drop. In fact, Guy Diamond actually dropped a hairpin, and everyone turned to say "Shhh!"

"Sorry," Guy whispered, carefully picking up the pin and holding it gently in both hands.

"I went out into the woods with Karma," Smidge explained. "She wanted to pick an extra-special flower to put in her hair for the big party tonight."

Everyone nodded. They knew Karma loved to weave all kinds of natural things into her hair—flowers, leaves, shells . . . even sticks. Once, Poppy had seen Karma try to balance a boulder in her hair, but it kept falling out.

"She led the way, since she knows all the secret paths through the forest," Smidge continued. "After a while, we found a field full of flowers that were different from any we'd ever seen before. They were so beautiful! And they smelled wonderful—almost as good as a fresh batch of spiced cupcakes!"

Several of the Trolls licked their lips. They could go for a warm cupcake right now! But then they'd miss the rest of Smidge's tale. . . .

"Karma decided to pick one of the strange flowers for her hair. But she wanted just the right one, the one that would look the best. She wandered deep into the field of flowers. They were so tall, I lost sight of her!" Smidge looked upset.

"That's all right, Smidge," Poppy said reassuringly. "Go on. Tell us what happened to Karma."

"I really don't know!" Smidge cried. "All I know is I heard this loud buzzing sound. It came, and then it went away. And when I looked for Karma, I couldn't find her anywhere! I shouted her name as loudly as I could, but she didn't answer!"

The Trolls looked concerned. When Smidge shouted, you answered. She was a very good shouter.

"Finally," Smidge said, "I ran back here to the village to get help!"

Poppy took Smidge's tiny hand. "You did

the right thing. We've got to find Karma. She may be in trouble!"

"But your hair isn't done yet!" Maddy protested. "In fact, I haven't even started on it. And I know you want it to be perfect for the party tonight."

"That's true, but some things are even more important than hair," Poppy said.

"Really?" Guy Diamond asked, amazed. "Are you sure about that?"

"Poppy's right," Maddy said, nodding. "I'll close the salon, and we'll go find Karma."

Poppy thought about it. "I don't think we *all* need to go. Just a small group. That way we'll travel faster, and it'll be easier to stick together."

With curlers still in his hair, Branch stood up. "I'll go," he said firmly.

"No," Poppy said, gently pushing him back into his chair. "You stay. It's your very first time in Maddy's salon! Maddy, you stay open and keep working on everyone's hair. It's what you do best! I'll go back into the forest with Smidge. DJ Suki, will you come with us? And Satin and Chenille?"

"Us two, too!" the twins agreed.

"Let's go!" DJ Suki cried. "I'm ready to drop the beat on this search!"

Poppy turned to her small friend. "Lead the way, Smidge!"

ℓℓℓℓℓℓℓℓ

At first, the five Trolls made good time through the woods. They were worried about Karma, and since it was a fine, sunny morning, there was nothing to slow them down. Tunebugs and Critterchords sang happy melodies in the sunshine.

But then the Trolls came to a fork in the path. Smidge, leading the way, stopped and stared at the two paths in front of her.

"What's wrong?" Poppy asked.

"I'm not sure which way to go," Smidge admitted. "When Karma and I were here before, I just followed her. You know how good she is at finding her way through the forest. She loves to explore."

"I know," Poppy said. "Nobody loves nature more than Karma."

"Well, do you have a *feeling*—" Satin began.

"—about which path might be the right one?" Chenille finished.

Smidge thought hard. Then she pointed to

the path on the left. "I think the field of flowers might be this way, but I'm really not sure."

"That's okay," Poppy said. "Let's try it! And if at some point you realize we're going in the wrong direction, we'll just turn around, come back, and try the other path. Okay? Come on!"

Poppy strode confidently down the left path. Smidge, Satin, Chenille, and DJ Suki followed her deeper and deeper into the forest.

Soon they found themselves in a part of the woods that was full of twigs. There were twigs on the ground. Twigs covering the path. Twigs hanging off branches. Twigs falling from the trees. It seemed to be *raining* twigs!

"There sure are a lot of twigs in this forest," Satin said.

DJ Suki jumped over a pile of twigs in the

path. "Don't *all* forests have twigs?" she asked.

"Sure," Chenille agreed. "But this has got to be the twiggiest forest I've ever seen!"

In no time at all, the Trolls' hair was full of twigs. As fast as they reached up to pluck them out, more twigs fell down and got tangled up in their locks.

"I've heard of sticky hair," Poppy said, trying to make a joke, "but this is ridiculous."

Suddenly, Smidge yelped, "Something just *flew* into my hair!"

"Let me guess," Satin said. "A twig?"

"No!" Smidge said. "Something ALIVE!"

Poppy ran over and parted Smidge's thick blue hair. Deep inside, she could see an odd little striped bird with a long beak and a short tail. "I see it!" she cried. "It looks like some kind of bird! But I've never seen one like it before."

"What's it doing in my hair?" Smidge cried. "Building a nest?"

Just then, the tiny bird flew out with a twig in its mouth. "It may be building a nest," Poppy said, "but not in your hair. It pulled out a twig!"

"That's good, I guess," Smidge said. "I wish it would pull them all out!"

DJ Suki squeaked. A little bird had flown into her hair, too! And another swept into Poppy's hair! When the birds emerged, they all had twigs in their mouths.

"It's okay," Poppy said, trying to calm down the other Trolls. "They just want to clean the twigs out of our hair. We should thank them!"

"I would," Chenille said, "but I don't speak Bird."

"I don't think this is the way Karma and I came," Smidge said, pulling another twig from her hair. "Maybe we should go back and try the other path."

Before Poppy could answer, a dark shadow passed over the trail. A bigger bird swooped down and grabbed a twig that was stuck in Satin and Chenille's joined hair. The big bird tried to yank the twig free, but the Trolls' hair was too thick. The twig was stuck. So the bird flew off with the twig in its mouth—carrying the twins high into the air!

"POPPY!" they screamed as they rose into the sky. "SAVE US!"

CHAPTER THREE

"WE'RE COMING!" Poppy shouted, racing off in the direction the bird had flown with the twins. Smidge and DJ Suki ran after her, leaping over piles of twigs, trying to keep up as best they could.

The twins' cries for help grew fainter and fainter.

Poppy kept looking up, trying to spot the

bird. More than once, she tripped over a twig and fell. But she got right back up and kept running.

Breathing hard, Poppy stopped for a moment and stared up at the tops of the tall trees. Where was the bird? And where were Satin and Chenille? Had the bird dropped them?

"There!" Smidge cried, pointing with her long blue hair. Poppy and DJ Suki looked to where the sharp-eyed little Troll was pointing, and they spotted the bird heading for the top of the tallest tree in the woods. They could just make out its nest, perched at the very pinnacle of the tree. The big bird landed in the nest and folded its wings.

"What's that bird doing with Satin and Chenille?" DJ Suki asked.

"I think she wanted the twig in their hair, not them," Poppy said. "It's hard to tell from down here, but I bet she's built her nest with twigs."

"I just hope she isn't planning to feed Satin and Chenille to her young," Smidge said. DJ Suki and Poppy stared at her with their mouths hanging open. What an awful thought!

"Come on!" Poppy cried. "We've got to climb that tree!"

The three Trolls ran as fast as they could to the base of the towering tree. They stood there, craning their necks, looking to the top.

It was an awfully long way.

DJ Suki jumped up and wrapped her arms around the trunk. She slowly slid right back down to the ground.

"This isn't going to be easy," she said

gloomily, plucking a splinter out of her rear end.

Poppy pointed at the lowest branch. "Smidge! You can use your hair to lift me up there!"

"If *you* believe it, *I* believe it!" Smidge said.

Poppy jumped on top of Smidge's hair. Using all her strength, the little Troll lifted her friend up to the branch.

"You did it!" Poppy shouted down. "Now it's DJ Suki's turn!"

Smidge quickly lifted DJ Suki up to the branch. Then Poppy and DJ Suki hauled Smidge up by her own hair. Once they were all on the branch, they could see that the branches above them were close together. Whipping their hair upward, they were able to lasso the higher branches and swing themselves up.

As they reached the higher branches of

the tree, the wind increased, making the trunk sway back and forth. "Hold on tight!" Poppy warned. "Wrap your hair all the way around each branch!"

"I'm swinging up, so you'd better get this rescue started!" DJ Suki sang as she made her way. The others laughed.

After climbing a few more branches, they saw it. The nest!

But were Satin and Chenille inside? Or had they been fed to the bird's hungry young babies?

"Satin!" Poppy hissed as quietly as she could, not wanting to get the big bird's attention. "Chenille! Are you in there?"

"Yes!" the twins hissed back quietly. "Get us out of here!"

Poppy, Smidge, and DJ Suki carefully

sneaked up to the bottom of the big nest. Poppy had been right—it was made of twigs.

"If we pull out some of these bottom twigs," Poppy whispered, "maybe we can make an escape hole for the twins."

They started yanking out twigs, letting them drop to the forest floor far below. Soon they'd opened up a hole big enough for a Troll to crawl through (as long as the Troll wasn't Biggie).

"Satin! Chenille!" Poppy whispered. "This way! Come on out!"

SQUAWK! The big bird stuck its long, sharp beak through the hole!

Without thinking, Smidge bellowed at the bird in her deep voice, "GO! GO! GET OUT OF HERE! YOU GO AWAY! NOW!"

At the same time, DJ Suki used two twigs

to beat on the trunk of the tree. She drummed out a dance beat: *THWACK, THWACK, THWACKATA, THWACKATA, THWACKATA, THWACK!*

Startled by the Trolls' screaming and drumming, the bird rose from her nest and flew away! Satin and Chenille scrambled down through the hole and out of the nest, dropping to the branch their friends were standing on.

"Thank you!" Satin exclaimed, hugging Poppy.

"We knew you wouldn't let us down!" Chenille added.

"No, but now we have to get out of this tree before that bird comes back," Poppy said, "and it's a long way to the ground!"

But by wrapping their hair around the next

branch down and then swinging to land on the one below it, the Trolls made quick progress out of the tree.

When they reached the lowest branch, Poppy jumped off and formed her hair into a staircase. She walked down the staircase to the ground, and the others followed. Soon all five of them were safely back on the floor of the forest.

The only problem was they were lost.

"How will we ever find Karma?" Smidge moaned, shaking her head.

"We'll find her!" Poppy promised. "Don't worry! Come on, let's go this way!" She walked confidently toward what seemed to be the lightest, brightest, friendliest part of the forest.

Gradually, as they marched along, the trees in the forest started to give way to huge mushrooms that towered over the Trolls. But even though the mushrooms were gigantic, they were comforting. Trolls loved mushrooms. They used them as chairs, sofas, umbrellas, tents—and even dance floors, in a pinch.

"Good ol' mushrooms," DJ Suki said, giving the trunk of a purple mushroom with sparkly gold stripes a friendly pat.

SCREEEECH!

The Trolls covered their ears. What was that?

The enormous mushroom reared back and gave another cry. *SCREEEECH!* The sound was echoed by the other mushrooms, and soon the air was filled with their deafening screeches!

"WHAT KIND OF MUSHROOMS ARE THESE?" Satin shouted into Poppy's ear.

"I THINK THEY MUST BE SCREECHING

MUSHROOMS!" Poppy yelled back.

"I'VE NEVER HEARD OF SCREECHING MUSHROOMS!" Chenille called.

"I NEVER WANT TO HEAR OF THEM AGAIN!" DJ Suki screamed.

Covering an ear with one hand and beckoning with her other hand, Poppy urged the Trolls to follow her out of the Forest of Screeching Mushrooms. "FOLLOW ME!" she shouted. "WE'VE GOT TO GET OUT OF HERE BEFORE WE LOSE OUR HEARING!"

As they ran past the thick stems of the giant mushrooms, the screeching seemed to get louder and louder. *SCREEECH! SCREEEECH! SCREEEEEEEEEECH!*

Finally, the Trolls left the last screeching mushroom behind. Exhausted and gasping, they collapsed onto soft, mossy mounds of dirt. They lay on the ground and cautiously took their hands off their ears. In the distance, they could hear the mushrooms' screeching start to die down.

"Smidge, do you remember coming upon those screeching mushrooms with Karma?" Poppy asked.

"Nope," Smidge said. "I think maybe I picked the wrong path!"

"What were those mushrooms so upset about?" DJ Suki asked.

"I guess they just REALLY—" Satin began.

"—don't like being patted!" Chenille finished.

The Trolls sat up and looked around. Now they weren't just lost. They were really, truly, *hopelessly* lost. "Which way should we go?" Satin asked.

"Well . . . ," Poppy said, trying to decide which direction looked best.

"May I help you?" a voice asked.

CHAPTER FOUR

"Who said that?" Poppy asked, looking around. All she saw was a small clump of dirt.

Then the clump of dirt moved toward them, and the Trolls realized it had a face, two arms, and two legs.

"Hi," said the clump of dirt in a friendly voice, waving hello. "I'm Clay."

"Okay," Satin said, "but what's your name?"

Clay winced. "Oh, I am *so* tired of that joke. Ever since the first day of Dirt School. Thanks so much, Mom and Dad, for naming me Clay."

"Sorry," Satin said. "I wasn't joking; I was just a little confused. So your *name* is Clay."

"Yes," Clay said, nodding his clumpy head.

Poppy walked right up to the strange little fellow and offered him her hand to shake. "Nice to meet you, Clay! I'm Poppy, and this is Satin, Chenille, DJ Suki, and Smidge."

Clay shook her hand. "Nice to meet you, too! We don't see many Trolls around this part of the forest." He leaned in and peered at their heads. "Especially with so many twigs in their hair."

"Speaking of Trolls," Poppy said, plucking out a long twig and tossing it aside, "did you happen to see another Troll today? She has long green hair with sticks and flowers in it."

"On purpose," Smidge added.

"And she's wearing a two-piece outfit," said Satin.

"Pale yellow, with a scalloped skirt," said Chenille.

"Cute material, and a nice design," Satin explained.

"*Really* cute," Chenille agreed. "We made it. You see, we've loved fashion since we were just little Trolls, so we decided to become clothing designers, and—"

"Have you seen her?" Poppy interrupted. "Her name's Karma, and she's missing."

Clay shook his head. "Nope. You're the first Trolls I've seen in ages. I'm sorry. I wish I knew where your missing friend is, but I haven't seen her. Where did you last see her?"

Smidge stepped forward. "It was in a field of tall, beautiful flowers. They smelled like spiced cupcakes, still warm from the oven."

"Do you have any idea where a field like that might be?" Poppy asked.

The little guy made out of dirt thought hard. Then he slowly started to nod. "Yes," he said. "Yes! I think I know the field you're talking about. Right now it's full of blooms. Beautiful flowers. Nice smell. Pretty colors."

Poppy was excited. "Could you please tell us the quickest way to get there?" she asked. "We're awfully worried about our friend."

Clay turned and pointed. "Do you see that stream over there? The fastest way to get to the field is to float down that stream."

"That's great!" Poppy cheered. "Can you come with us and show us the way?"

Clay looked nervous. He shook his head rapidly from side to side. "N-n-no!" he stammered. "I couldn't do that! No!"

"Why not?" DJ Suki asked curiously.

"Because," he explained, looking a little embarrassed, "I never travel on water. I might fall in. When I fall into water, I become . . . muddy. And I do *not* like to be muddy! I just . . . go all to pieces!"

Clay was clearly upset at the thought of falling into a stream. Poppy touched his arm softly to reassure him. "That's okay," she said. "You don't have to come. We're very grateful for the information you've given us! You've been terrific!"

"I have?" Clay said, brightening. He stood up straight. "Thank you! Come with me—I'll show you some good leaves for building boats! I mean, I *assume* they're good for building boats. I've never built one myself." He paused. "Boats." He shuddered.

"Thank you!" Poppy said. "Lead on!"

Clay led the way to the stream. Before they reached the water, he showed the Trolls a plant with big, shiny green leaves. "These are perfect for making boats, I'm told. They're strong, but they float and keep the water out."

DJ Suki climbed up the plant, shinnied out to the end of a stem, and put her full weight on it until a leaf in front of her touched the ground. Smidge used her great strength to pluck the leaf off the stem. *SPROING!* The stem sprang up and whipped back and forth with DJ Suki holding on for dear life.

"WHOOOAH!" she cried.

Working together, the Trolls picked enough leaves to make two boats.

"But how will we put the leaves together?" Poppy asked.

"I know!" Satin said. "We'll SEW them together!"

"Great idea!" Chenille said. "I always carry a couple of needles with me, just in case." She pulled out her handy portable sewing kit. "What'll we use for thread?"

The Trolls were stumped for a second. Then Clay shyly suggested, "Your hair?" Since he didn't have much experience with Trolls, he wasn't sure if the suggestion would offend them. But their hair looked strong—perfect for lashing some leaves together to make two small boats.

"Great!" Poppy said. "Smidge, is it all right if we use your hair? It's the longest and strongest."

"Be my guest," Smidge said in her deep voice. She plucked several long blue hairs from her head and handed them to Satin and Chenille. They threaded the hairs through the eyes of their needles and swiftly sewed the shiny green leaves together. Soon they had two boats for the five Trolls to float in.

As they carried their boats to the water, Clay said, "When the stream splits in two, make sure you go to the right. That way will take you to the flower field. The other way won't!"

"Got it!" Poppy said. "Go to the right!"

"How are we going to steer our boats?" DJ Suki asked.

"Good question," Poppy said. "I think we need to make oars."

The Trolls looked around for the right material. Smidge spotted a tree with the kind of bark they needed—curved and strong, but not so strong that they couldn't snap it into Troll-sized oars. They broke off some bark and adjusted the pieces.

With Clay at a safe distance, they found a good spot along the stream to launch their boats. Poppy and the twins climbed into one boat, while DJ Suki and Smidge got in the other. They pushed off from the bank and were quickly swept downstream by the flowing water.

As they steered with their oars, they called to Clay, "Thank you! Thank you so much for all your help!"

"You're welcome!" he called, cupping his dirt hands around his dirt mouth. "And remember: KEEP TO THE RIGHT!"

The water was moving fast, so the Trolls made great time.

"Whoo-hoo!" Poppy said. "This sure beats walking!"

As they skimmed along in their leaf boats, the Trolls enjoyed the spray of water and the rush of air blowing their hair back.

"Sweet!" DJ Suki shouted.

But then they noticed that the water was starting to flow faster. And faster, and faster . . .

CHAPTER FIVE

WHOOSH! The Trolls' little boats were suddenly zooming through white-water rapids! As they bounced up and down, water splashed into their boats. Using their paddles, they worked hard to keep from capsizing.

"Now I know why Clay never got into this stream!" Satin shouted over the roar of the rapids.

"He never went into ANY stream!" Chenille

yelled. "He had no idea what this would be like!"

"Try to steer toward the calmest part of the water!" Poppy called out to her boatmates.

"*What* calm part?" Chenille asked. "It all looks wild to me!"

As they struggled to keep their boats upright in the churning water, DJ Suki and Smidge were swept ahead of Poppy, Satin, and Chenille. With only two Trolls in it—one of them very small— DJ Suki and Smidge's boat was much lighter than Poppy, Satin, and Chenille's.

"Stay together!" Poppy called to Smidge and DJ Suki. "We've got to stay together!"

"But how?" Satin asked. "We forgot to put brakes on our boats!"

Poppy and the twins watched helplessly as

DJ Suki and Smidge's boat swiftly approached the split Clay had told them about. To their dismay, the boat was swept to the left! It passed the split and zoomed down the left channel!

"But that dirt guy said to go to the right!" Chenille shouted.

"I don't think they had any choice," Poppy said. "The current is too strong. They just got carried off to the left. Which means *we've* gotta go to the left, too! We can't abandon our friends!"

All three Trolls pushed their oars into the water, steering their boat to the left. But it wasn't really necessary. The water was pulling them straight toward the left channel of the stream anyway. When they reached the split, they were nowhere near the right channel.

"So much for our quick and easy path to the flower field!" Satin said. "Maybe we should have asked the dirt guy what *this* way leads to!"

Poppy craned her neck to peer around the spray of white water coming off their bow. "Can you see Smidge and DJ Suki's boat?" she asked the twins.

"There!" Chenille cried, pointing. "I saw them just for a second, before the stream bent. They're not too far ahead of us!"

"Then let's try to catch up," Poppy said. "Paddle!"

The three Trolls paddled as hard as they could. Even though the water was still moving fast, their paddling made a difference. They sped up, and before too long, Poppy shouted, "We're catching up!"

"WATCH OUT FOR THAT BOULDER!" Satin and Chenille screamed.

Poppy had been so intent on spotting Smidge and DJ Suki that she didn't notice a big rock rising out of the water right in front of them.

The three Trolls dove for the left side of the boat, leaning as far as they could without tipping it over. They swerved left, just barely missing the rock. The leaf boat scraped against the rock's rough surface, but it didn't tear, and the stitches made with Smidge's hair held—for the moment.

"Whew!" Poppy gasped. "That was WAY too close!"

In the front boat, Smidge and DJ Suki had been glancing back to search for the other boat whenever they could take their eyes off the rough water. They were worried that Poppy and the twins hadn't followed them when they were swept into the left channel of the raging stream.

"There they are!" Smidge bellowed. "They almost hit the same rock we almost hit!"

"POPPY! SATIN! CHENILLE!" DJ Suki yelled. "CATCH UP TO US! WE'LL TRY TO SLOW DOWN!"

The boats didn't have brakes, so the Trolls used the oars to paddle against the force of the stream. Finally, Poppy's boat caught up, and the two boats were side by side again.

"I'm so glad to see you!" Poppy cried.

"Sorry we went the wrong way," DJ Suki said. "The current was too strong."

"I know," Poppy said. "It was too strong for us, too. But the important thing is that we're back together, so there's nothing to worry about."

"Actually, there is," Satin and Chenille said, pointing.

Farther downstream, they heard the roar of crashing water that could only mean . . .

CHAPTER SIX

"A waterfall!" Satin shouted.

"WE'RE ALL GONNA DIE!" Chenille screamed.

"Oh, no we're not!" Poppy said confidently. "Paddle! Paddle as hard as you can! We've got to get to the shore before we reach that waterfall!"

The five Trolls paddled like mad, steering their boats toward the left bank. The water was still moving quickly, sweeping toward the waterfall. They could hear the roar of the falls, and they saw a thick mist rising from the churning rapids far below.

In fact, it was so misty that their hair was soaked and drooping over their faces. They had to keep pushing it out of their eyes so they could see where they were going.

"Lean left!" Poppy said. "That'll help steer the boats!"

DJ Suki leaned so far to the left, she almost fell into the water! Smidge whipped her wet hair around her friend's waist and yanked. Lucky for DJ Suki, Smidge was strong enough to pull her back into the boat.

"Thanks!" DJ Suki gasped.

"Don't mention it!" Smidge bellowed.

Poppy, Satin, and Chenille paddled their leaf boat as hard as they could. They were getting closer to the shore, but they were also still moving downstream, toward the roaring falls. Poppy spotted a tree leaning over the water and had an idea.

"Smidge!" she shouted. "Try to grab that branch with your hair and pull yourself in! You've got the longest hair, and you're the strongest! If any Troll can do it, you can!"

"If *you* believe, *I* believe!" Smidge shouted back. She swung her wet blue hair around in the air three times, spraying them all with water. Then she whipped her hair toward the branch. *WHAP!* It hit the branch and wrapped around. Smidge grabbed her hair and started pulling, hand over hand, hauling their boat toward the shore. "Grab on to our boat!" she yelled to the three Trolls in the other leaf boat.

To free their hands, Poppy, Satin, and Chenille dropped their oars into the water. Bobbing and sinking, the pieces of bark shot downstream and over the falls, out of sight. The three Trolls reached toward the other boat, grabbing the stern. Poppy was practically pulled out of their boat—her toes were hooked over the edge!

"Should we climb into their boat?" Satin shouted.

"It won't hold all five of us!" Poppy yelled back. "Just stay in our boat and hold on to theirs!"

"Smidge had better hurry!" Chenille shouted. "The stitches holding the leaves together are starting to come apart!"

"I'M HURRYING!" Smidge bellowed. "HOLD ON TO EACH OTHER'S FEET!"

DJ Suki grabbed Smidge's feet. Poppy grabbed DJ Suki's feet, and Satin grabbed Poppy's feet just as Chenille grabbed Satin's. It was a Troll chain!

Just as the two boats were about to be swept over the falls, Smidge gave a mighty tug on her own hair, yanking them all onto the bank. They flopped to the grass like fish out of water.

For a moment, they just lay there, panting. "Great job, Smidge," Poppy gasped. "Thanks."

"You're welcome," Smidge panted.

"Well done, everybody," DJ Suki said. "I can't believe the boats held together in rapids."

"They wouldn't have lasted much longer," Chenille said.

"You're right," Satin agreed. "Look."

She pointed to the stream below the waterfall. The boats had broken apart, and the shiny green leaves were floating on the water. The Trolls watched the leaves spin around and slip past the rocks. A big fish came to the surface and swallowed one of the leaves whole. *GULP!*

"Okay!" Poppy said, standing up and shaking the water out of her hair like a dog. "Let's go find Karma! I'll bet we can still get back in time for the party tonight!"

The other Trolls exchanged looks. In all the excitement, they'd forgotten about the party. It seemed impossible that they'd ever be able to rescue Karma and find their way back to Troll Village in time for the celebration.

But as always, Poppy stayed positive. "Come

on!" she said, helping the others to their feet. "All we have to do is find that field of flowers. Maybe Karma's waiting there for us. By now she's found the perfect flower for her hair. Wait'll she sees *our* hair!"

The Trolls looked at each other's hair, wet and full of twigs, and started to laugh.

"Let's go *this* way!" Poppy urged. "I've got a good feeling about this direction!"

"I wish I could say the same thing," Chenille muttered to Satin.

As they made their way through the woods, DJ Suki spotted something up ahead. "Look over there! Isn't that some kind of field?"

"Of flowers?" Poppy asked, excited.

"I'm not sure," DJ Suki said. "Let's run!"

But Poppy was already running, eager to see if they'd found the field of beautiful flowers Smidge had described. She dodged trees and jumped over fallen branches, hurrying to reach the field just beyond the trees. "KARMA!" she shouted as she ran. "KARMA, WHERE ARE YOU?"

She passed the last tree and saw a field, but it wasn't full of flowers. "I don't see any blooms," she said, disappointed. There were only plants. Their leaves were bright red, orange, and yellow, but they had no flowers or petals.

DJ Suki caught up and stood beside her. "Are you sure?" she asked. "Let's look a little closer." She stepped into the field of plants, searching for flowers, and . . .

SPROING! Suddenly, DJ Suki shot up into

the air! "DJ!" Poppy cried. She ran forward, and . . . *SPROING!*

Poppy was sent soaring high into the sky, too!

When Satin, Chenille, and Smidge ran into the field to see what was going on . . .

SPROING! SPROING! SPROING! All three bounced into the air!

The plants they'd stepped on were Spring Plants—not plants that grow in the spring (though they sometimes do, which is a little confusing), but plants that act like springs. If someone steps on a Spring Plant, it throws the stepper high into the air!

Unfortunately, when Poppy fell back down, she landed right on another Spring Plant! *SPROING!*

"AAAAAH!" Poppy yelled when she was flung into the air again.

"WHAAAAH!" DJ Suki screamed as she bounced from plant to plant.

The others were yelling, too: "YAAAH!" "HEYYYYY!" "NOOOOO!"

Poppy tried to make a staircase out of her hair, but because she was tumbling upside down, it was hard for her to aim her hair at the ground. Then, when she finally managed to aim her hair, it set off another Spring Plant, which sent her hair flying right back into her face!

SPROING! SPROING! SPROING!

If anyone had been around to witness the scene, it might have looked as though the Trolls were bouncing on dozens of trampolines—

moving from one trampoline to the next, spinning and somersaulting through the air. It would have made a pretty decent circus act. But unfortunately, the entire operation was out of their control.

Finally, each Troll was sprung past the edge of the Spring Plants field, where they landed on bare ground. *THUMP! WHUMP! WHOMP! THWOMP! THUMP!* The five Trolls lay in a heap.

"Okay, so they're not flowers," DJ Suki said.

"Actually," Poppy said, "that was kind of fun! And it was a quick way to get across the field. Now let's see which way we should go. I guess I should have tried to look around while I was up in the air, but it was hard when I was tumbling upside down." She stood up and peered into the distance, shading her eyes with her hand.

Chenille sniffed. "Does anyone else smell something weird?"

The others sniffed and nodded. "Definitely," Smidge said in her bass voice.

Poppy took a step, and . . .

CHAPTER SEVEN

SHPLORP.

Poppy's foot sank into the wet ground. She pulled her foot out. *SHHHPLOOP!* A greasy gob dripped from it. "This is a marsh!" she cried. "A greasy marsh!"

"Yuck!" Satin said, lifting her foot out of the gooey ground. "This stinks. Literally."

"Well, we can't go back through that field with all the bouncy plants," Poppy said. "We've got to go on. Let's just hope this marshland ends soon."

SHPLORP. SHPLOOP. SHPLOP. SHWURK. The Trolls walked as best they could through the greasy swamp, pulling their feet out of the muck with each step. They kept their eyes peeled for stepping-stones, but there weren't any.

Unfortunately, the grease wasn't just under their feet. The swamp trees had long, mossy branches that hung almost to the ground, dripping with more grease—which dripped right into the Trolls' hair.

"Well," Poppy said, trying to look on the bright side, "maybe with all this grease in our hair, the twigs will slide out."

Satin giggled. "Hee hee hee!"

So did Chenille. "Heh heh heh!"

DJ Suki giggled, too. "Tee-hee hee hee!"

Smidge giggled the lowest, deepest giggles they'd ever heard. "Ho ho! Hoo hoo hoo!"

"Why are we laughing?" said Poppy, chuckling. "Did I say something really funny?"

"Hee hee—no," Satin managed to say between giggles. "Walking—hee hee hee!—through this greasy swamp . . . heh heh! . . . doesn't seem at all funny."

"But I can't help giggling!" Chenille tittered.

"It's like—hee hee!—we're being tickled!" DJ Suki chuckled.

Suddenly, Poppy remembered something. "I think this must be the Tickle Marsh. I've heard of it, but I've never been here. Hee hee hee!"

"What's a Tickle Marsh?" Smidge asked.

"My dad told me about it, heh heh heh,"

Poppy said. Her dad was King Peppy. "He found it a long time ago, when he was looking for a place for us to live. Hee hee hee! The ooze in the swamp has this weird effect on anyone who gets it on them. Hee hee! It tickles!"

Satin looked down at her feet. They were covered with ooze. "Heh heh—well, we've certainly got it on us. Hee hee! On our feet, in our hair . . . and even though I'm laughing—hee hee hee hee—it's not funny!"

The giggling was getting exhausting. Their stomachs were starting to hurt. The five Trolls ran, eager to escape from the Tickle Marsh. But it wasn't easy running through a swamp. *SPLAT!* DJ Suki tripped and fell facedown in the mucky ooze. When she lifted her greasy face, she was still giggling. "Hee hee hee hee!"

Finally, after what seemed like ages but was really only a few minutes, they reached the edge of the marsh, where the ground was more solid. They ran on dry grass, then collapsed, wiped out from all the giggling.

"I usually love laughing"—Poppy gasped—"but that was weird."

"I agree," DJ Suki said. "Nobody say anything funny."

Unfortunately, that struck Satin and Chenille as funny, and they started to laugh again. Smidge, Poppy, and even DJ Suki couldn't help joining in.

"My aching stomach!" Chenille complained, still laughing.

Satin tried to run her fingers through their hair. "How are we ever going to get all this grease out of our hair?" she asked.

"Not to mention the twigs," Smidge said.

Poppy glanced around and saw they were in an open, rocky field. There weren't any flowers, so she knew it wasn't the field Smidge had been in when Karma disappeared. But at least it looked much easier to walk through than the greasy Tickle Marsh.

As they lay there trying to recover their strength, the Trolls felt a breeze. It felt good, and it smelled fresh after the stench of the marsh. But the breeze picked up, blowing harder, until the breeze became a wind.

And then the wind blew harder, and harder . . .

CHAPTER EIGHT

Poppy jumped to her feet. "We'd better hurry! I feel a big storm coming!"

They all got up and started walking. They hadn't taken more than a few steps when . . . *WHOOSH!* A gust of wind picked up Smidge, spinning her around and lifting her high into the air! It was a mini tornado!

"WHOOOOOAH!" she bellowed. "HELP!"

But the four other Trolls were too busy dealing with their own mini tornados to help Smidge. One twisted Satin and Chenille's hair into a terrible tangle. Another blew DJ Suki across the field. And a third picked up Poppy and flung her even higher into the sky than Smidge!

Poppy looked down and saw that the field was full of mini tornados—spinning cyclones that skimmed around the meadow, bumping into each other and flying off in opposite directions. Poppy was spinning so fast that she was getting dizzy.

WHUMP! Poppy was set back down on the ground. "Try to stay together!" she shouted to the others. "We can't get separated!"

Another tiny twister picked up Satin and

Chenille, spinning them off the ground. They didn't go too high—about as high as three Trolls standing on each other's shoulders—but they spun around at a terrific speed. The twins managed to join hands while their feet stuck straight out behind them as they twirled around like a pinwheel.

WHOMP! Smidge landed back on the ground. "Whew!" she groaned. "That's enough of tha—" But before she could finish, another mini tornado whirled her up again, carrying her even higher than before. "I DON'T LIKE THIS!" she wailed.

DJ Suki didn't get lifted high into the air, but the mini tornados spun her all over the field. She was like a ballet dancer forced into pirouettes. She was getting so dizzy, she was afraid she'd toss her cupcakes! "Make . . . it . . . stop!" she moaned. "I want to get off this ride!"

WHAM! Satin and Chenille crashed to the ground, still holding hands.

"You okay?" Satin asked her twin.

"I think so," Chenille answered, "but our hair is a mess!"

Poppy got an idea. Maybe if the five Trolls joined hands, together they would be too heavy for the mini tornados to lift off the ground. But first they had to get close enough to each other to reach.

"Everyone get together!" Poppy shouted to the others. "We'll join hands! Maybe all together we can keep ourselves from being blown away! It'll be like Hug Time!"

Since Satin and Chenille were already

holding hands, Poppy decided to try to make her way over to them. She put her head down and dug in, walking into the fierce wind, resisting its attempt to pull her up into a funnel cloud.

But the strong wind kept lifting Poppy off her feet. She thought if she stayed close to the ground, she could avoid the gusts, so she got down on her hands and knees and crawled toward the twins.

Smidge saw Poppy slowly heading toward Satin and Chenille. The little Troll decided to use the strength of her long hair to reach them. She swung her head in a circle, whipping her blue hair around three times, then snapped it forward, aiming for one of Chenille's legs. On her first two tries, the wind blew her hair off course, but the third time, her hair wrapped around Satin's leg. "Close enough!" Smidge said, slowly pulling herself toward the twins.

Once Poppy and Smidge got to Satin and Chenille, they all grabbed on to each other, holding tight in the howling wind. They tried moving a few cautious steps together. The mini tornados weren't lifting them off the ground!

"It's working!" Satin and Chenille cried.

"Let's try to walk over to DJ Suki!" Poppy shouted.

"Where is she?" Smidge asked.

They looked around and saw that DJ Suki was still spinning around the field, carried from one spot to another by the tiny twisters. Every time the clump of four Trolls tried to reach her, she went whirling off in another direction.

"DJ!" Poppy yelled. "Try to hold on to

something! Anything! Then we'll come to you!"

"I'll try!" DJ Suki yelled back. "But I don't know what to hold on to! This field's pretty bare! I think everything's been blown away!"

As the mini tornados spun her around the field, DJ Suki frantically looked for something. There were no trees. No bushes. No rocks. Just hard-packed dirt.

But then she spotted something sticking out of the ground—a gnarled old root.

DJ Suki crawled over to the root. She grabbed it and hung on with all her might, hoping it wouldn't come loose. Thankfully, even when a twister lifted her feet off the ground, she was able to hold on to the old root.

Poppy saw that DJ Suki had managed to stay in one spot. "This way!" she shouted over the roaring wind. "She's right over there!"

The huddle of Trolls slowly shuffled toward DJ Suki. Their long hair whipped around their heads, sometimes slapping one of them in the face. *WHAP!*

When they reached DJ Suki, Poppy yelled, "Grab on to us!"

"I'm afraid to let go of this root!" DJ Suki admitted.

"It'll be okay!" Poppy said. "We'll catch you!"

Just as DJ Suki let go of the root and stretched her arm toward the cluster of Trolls, a gust of wind picked her up and spun her around again! But Smidge shot out an arm, grabbed DJ Suki's foot, and pulled her into their desperate group hug. Poppy was so relieved, she hugged DJ

Suki for real. "I'm so glad you're okay."

Now that the five Trolls were bunched together, they couldn't be lifted up and spun around by the tornados. Holding each other tightly and shuffling along, they made their way toward the edge of the gusty field.

"Almost there . . . ," Satin said.

"Just a few more steps . . . ," Chenille added.

Poppy had an idea. "Wait," she said. "Even when we get out of this blowy field, we won't know which way to go."

The others were puzzled. This didn't sound like Poppy. It didn't sound positive.

"Well," DJ Suki said uncertainly, "we'll figure something out."

"Let me go," Poppy said. "I'll let one of the twisters lift me up, and then I'll have a good look around. From up high, maybe I'll be able to spot the flower field!"

"Or maybe you'll get blown away!" Satin said.

"We can't let you go!" Chenille agreed. "It's way too dangerous!"

"I have an idea," Smidge said. "I'll hold on to Poppy with my hair. You all hold on to me. *Then* we'll let the tornado carry her up. It'll be like flying a kite!"

DJ Suki looked doubtful. "Except Poppy's not a kite. She's a Troll."

"I think it's a great idea!" Poppy said. "Let's do it!"

Smidge wrapped the ends of her hair around Poppy's ankle. The clump of Trolls shuffled a few steps back into the field of tornados. Then they let go of Poppy. She took a step or two away from the huddle . . . and was twisted up into the air!

"Here I GO!" Poppy shouted, spinning away from them.

She quickly rose as high as Smidge's hair would let her. Smidge's hair stretched and stretched until *she* started to rise off the ground—but the other three Trolls clutched her feet tightly.

At first, Poppy was spinning so fast that everything looked like a blur. But then she got used to the twirling and was able to focus on what she had spotted in the distance down below. Poppy saw the edge of the field, and a forest, and a stream, and . . . a field of flowers!

"I SEE IT!" Poppy yelled, but the wind

was so loud, the others couldn't hear her. She signaled to them with frantic hand gestures to pull her down.

"What's she saying?" Satin asked.

"I think she's ready to come down," DJ Suki guessed.

"Okay, Smidge," Chenille said. "Reel her in! Time to land this Troll!"

With a tremendous effort, Smidge tugged on her hair and managed to haul Poppy down to the ground through the roaring, swirling wind. When Poppy was within reach, the Trolls pulled her into their huddle.

"Did you see it?" DJ Suki asked.

"Yes!" Poppy said, breathing hard. "I saw the field of flowers!"

CHAPTER NINE

"We still have to get out of this tornado field," Poppy said. "Let's head to the nearest edge, and then I'll show you which way I think we should go."

Still in their hug formation, the five Trolls carefully shuffled across the bare ground to the edge of the field. They stepped onto some grass, and the winds immediately died down.

"Well, we got out of that field," Satin said, "but I don't know if we'll ever get all these tangles out of our hair." They looked at the mess on top of each other's heads. The tornados had whipped their hair into crazy knots and snarls.

"At least the knots will hold in the twigs and the grease," Chenille said.

"How is *that* good?" her twin sister asked.

"Just trying to be positive," Chenille said, shrugging.

"Okay, Poppy," DJ Suki said, "which way to the flower field?"

Poppy pointed. "That way. Straight through the forest. On the other side of the woods, I saw a stream. I think it might be the one we were in before, the stream that Clay said would lead right to the field of flowers."

"All right!" Smidge said. "What are we waiting for? Let's get through that forest!"

They walked into the woods. There wasn't a path, but the ground didn't have much growing out of it besides trees. The only thing they saw on the ground was nuts.

Lots of nuts.

BONK! A nut fell right on Poppy's head! Luckily, her hair was so matted and clumpy, the nut bounced right off.

"That's funny," she said to the others. "A nut just fell right on my head! What are the odds?"

BONK! BONK! BONK!

Nuts fell onto the others' heads, too! Except Smidge's. She laughed. "I guess I'm the only one who hasn't had a nut fall on—" *BONK!* A big nut clonked her right on the head. "Ow!"

As they walked deeper into the forest, the nuts fell faster and got bigger. It seemed to be raining nuts!

"Ouch!" DJ Suki said. "This has to be the nuttiest forest I've ever walked through!"

"Let's make it the nuttiest forest we've ever *run* through!" Satin suggested.

They started running through the storm of nuts. But it wasn't easy, since the trees in the Forest of Falling Nuts had big, gnarled roots that curved up out of the ground. The Trolls had to either leap over the roots or duck under them. And more than once, they tripped and fell.

Many nuts were lodged in their hair, joining the twigs and the grease.

After tripping yet again, Chenille grew so frustrated, she looked up at the trees to scream,

"Stop dropping all your nuts on us!" But her mouth quickly filled with nuts. She spat them out. *"PTOOEY!"*

Following right behind her attached twin, Satin stepped on the nuts and found herself running in place for a minute on the slippery pile Chenille had spat out. Chenille kept moving, so eventually Satin was jerked off her makeshift treadmill.

Feeling battered, the Trolls reached the edge of the Forest of Falling Nuts. A clear stream ran between the forest and the field of flowers.

Poppy pointed across the stream at the field. "Is that it, Smidge? Is that the field where you went with Karma so she could pick a flower for her hair?"

Smidge peered at the blooming field.

She smiled. "Yes!" she bellowed. "That's it! KARMA! ARE YOU OVER THERE?"

There was no answer.

"We've got to get across this stream and search that field," Poppy said determinedly.

They looked at the stream. The water was flowing steadily, but not as swiftly as it had been before. It made a pleasant gurgling sound as it rippled through the stones and tree roots.

"Could we swim across?" DJ Suki said. "It doesn't look dangerous."

Poppy considered the suggestion. "I suppose we could, but I'd hate to risk anything bad happening to one of us. Remember that big fish we saw that ate the leaf from our boat?"

The others nodded. They remembered the fish with its big mouth, the perfect size for swallowing a Troll in a single bite. It wasn't pleasant to think about a fish like that lurking in the shadowy depths of this stream.

Smidge had an idea. "How about a zoom rope?" she suggested.

CHAPTER TEN

"A zoom rope!" Poppy enthused. "That's a GREAT idea!"

Trolls loved to string a rope between two trees and flip their hair over it, then grab the ends of their hair and slide down. They usually rode zoom ropes for fun and transport around Troll Village, but it could also be a handy way to cross a stream full of hungry fish.

"What'll we use for the rope?" DJ Suki asked.

"Our hair's way too messed up with sticks and nuts and grease—" Satin started.

"—for us to make a rope long enough to cross this stream," Chenille finished.

Poppy nodded. "That's true. But maybe we can find a vine."

"Back in that forest with all the nuts bonking us on the head?" Chenille asked, making a face.

"Let's look around," Poppy suggested. "Maybe we can find a vine without getting bonked again."

They scanned the ground and nearby trees.

"Found one!" Satin said, pointing at a tree near the stream. A vine dangled from a branch high above them.

"And it looks long enough!" Chenille added.

"Smidge, do you think you could pull that vine down?" Poppy asked.

"You got it," Smidge said, spitting on her hands and rubbing them together. She strode over to the vine, jumped up, and gave it a good strong yank. The vine fell at her feet, piling itself into a neat coil.

"Chenille, Satin—with all your sewing, you're the experts at tying knots," Poppy said, handing them the vine. "Can you tie the right kind of knot for us to lasso a tree branch across the stream?"

"Totes!" Chenille exclaimed.

"No doubt!" Satin agreed. The twins went to work and tied a perfect lasso onto the end of the vine.

Since Smidge was the strongest, they picked her to toss the vine across the stream. She swung the vine around her head three times and then threw it at a branch on the other side.

She missed.

"That's okay!" Poppy said, clapping her hands. "Try it again! The first throw's just for measuring the distance, anyway."

With a quick flick of her wrist, Smidge snapped the vine back to their side of the stream. Then she swung it around her head again and whipped it at the thick broken branch across the water.

The vine lasso looped around the branch!

"All right! Way to go, Smidge!" the other Trolls cheered.

Smidge pulled on the vine, and the twins'

knot tightened and held. Holding the other end, she quickly climbed a tree on their side of the stream and tied it to a sturdy branch.

The zoom rope was ready.

ZOOM! ZOOM! ZOOM! One at a time, the Trolls flipped their hair over the line, grabbed on to it, and slid to the other side of the stream.

Poppy went last. As she zipped over the middle of the creek, a big fish leapt out of the water, snapping its jaws at her feet! "YAAAH!" Poppy screamed, lifting her feet as high as she could.

SPLASH! The big fish flopped back into the stream, spraying water to the bank and soaking the other Trolls. Poppy dropped to the grass, shaking a little from her close call with the leaping fish.

"*Really* glad we didn't try to swim across," Chenille said.

Poppy didn't stay shaken for long. She walked toward the field of flowers.

"KARMA!" she called. "WHERE ARE YOU?"

They all shouted Karma's name as they made their way deeper into the field.

But there was no answer.

"Are you sure this is the right field of flowers, Smidge?" Poppy asked.

"Positive!" Smidge insisted. "And that's the buzzing I heard just before Karma disappeared!"

They all heard it—a buzzing that got louder and louder . . .

"Where is that noise coming from?" DJ Suki asked.

"There!" Chenille shouted, pointing to the sky.

It was a huge Stingerbug, bigger than three Trolls put together! Bigger than Biggie! And it was diving straight at them! *BZZZZZ!*

"HIT THE DIRT!" Smidge yelled. The Trolls dove just as the Stingerbug swooped down where they'd been standing. Just before he reached the ground, he pulled up, climbing back into the sky.

But he circled around again.

"HERE HE COMES!" Satin warned.

The Stingerbug went into another deep dive. *BZZZZZZ!* He was heading right for them!

"Spread out!" Chenille hissed. "Hide!"

The Trolls separated, scrambling to hide underneath the tall flowers. The Stingerbug skimmed the tops of the flowers, just inches above the Trolls' heads. His buzz was furiously loud. *BZZZZZZ!*

"This is ridiculous!" Poppy said, standing up. "I'm not hiding anymore!"

Overhead, the gigantic flying creature was preparing to dive at the Trolls again.

"Poppy, get down!" Satin whispered. "That thing'll sting you, or bite you, or knock your head off!"

"Or maybe," she said bravely, "it'll answer my questions!"

She looked up at the diving critter, cupped her hands around her mouth, and called, "Hello! My name is Poppy! Why are you trying to drive us away? And have you seen our friend Karma?"

The huge bug pulled up abruptly and hovered

over Poppy, still buzzing angrily. "Begone!" it commanded. "Access to this place is strictly restricted! You have no right to be here!"

Poppy looked confused. "No right to be in a field full of beautiful flowers? Why?"

"Because," the Stingerbug growled, "these beautiful flowers belong to the queen! You are FORBIDDEN to walk among them! And you are ABSOLUTELY FORBIDDEN to pick them! Anyone caught picking these flowers will be carried off to the palace!"

"That must be what happened to Karma!" Smidge whispered. "She probably picked a flower!"

That gave Poppy an idea. Staring defiantly into the Stingerbug's big dark eyes, she reached out and seized the stem of the nearest tall flower.

The Stingerbug looked alarmed. "Don't you dare!" he warned.

SNAP! Poppy picked the flower!

The critter gasped! "You dare?"

"Oh, yeah," Poppy said calmly, "I dare."

The other Trolls exchanged a quick look. Following Poppy's lead, they each picked a flower and pulled. *SNAP! SNAP! SNAP! SNAP!*

"THAT'S IT!" the Stingerbug roared. "YOU'RE ALL GOING TO THE PALACE!"

At the sound of his buzz, now louder and higher-pitched, four more Stingerbugs swooped in over the field. The first Stingerbug picked up Poppy, and the new arrivals swept up Satin, Chenille, DJ Suki, and Smidge.

They were all headed to the palace—which was exactly what Poppy wanted.

CHAPTER ELEVEN

The Stingerbug queen's palace hung high in the branches of an enormous tree. As the Stingerbugs carried them up to it, the Trolls saw that the palace was shaped like a Troll pod, only upside down, with the thickest part at the top and the pointy part at the bottom. But it wasn't soft and colorful. The palace looked as if it were made from a hard, drab-colored material, like dried mud. And it was much, much bigger than any Troll pod.

"Some palace," Chenille murmured to Satin.

"They could definitely use some help with their design and outside decor," Satin agreed.

The Stingerbugs flew through an arched entrance near the bottom of the palace. Once inside, they flew through long, wide halls, which were filled with buzzing bugs.

"Make way! Make way!" the biggest Stingerbug growled. "We are carrying prisoners for the queen! FLOWER-PICKERS!"

Angry buzzes of disapproval came from the Stingerbug crowd.

At the top of the palace, the Stingerbugs flew past some guards and into the queen's royal chamber. The queen was not present. The

Stingerbugs put the Trolls down and ushered them into a cage. As the cage door slammed closed behind them, the Trolls saw . . . Karma!

"Karma!" they cried. "Are you all right?"

"Poppy! Smidge! DJ Suki! Satin! Chenille!" Karma called joyfully as she ran over and hugged them. "Yes, I'm all right! But these Stingerbugs are very mad at me for picking one of their flowers."

"They're mad at us, too," Poppy said.

"Why?" Karma asked.

"Same reason," Poppy said. "But don't worry. We're going to get out of here!"

"How?" Karma asked.

Poppy hesitated. She didn't actually know *how* the Trolls would escape the Stingerbugs' palace, but she was confident that they would.

"ALL RISE FOR THE QUEEN!" one of the Stingerbugs ordered. The Stingerbugs in the royal chamber vibrated their transparent wings, rising slightly off the floor.

The queen flew into the chamber.

She was even bigger than the Stingerbugs who had carried the Trolls to the palace. She wore a long, dark cape decorated with the petals of the same flowers the Trolls had picked. The Trolls could see a long, sharp stinger behind her cape.

"The queen rules over these Stingerbugs," Karma told the other Trolls. "They do whatever she says. It's a fascinating system. I don't know whether she's elected, or inherits the throne—"

"SILENCE!" roared a Stingerbug.

The queen took her place on a throne next

to a large column that had fallen to the floor. The Stingerbug who had first dive-bombed the Trolls in the flower field approached the throne.

"Your Majesty," he buzzed. "We present to you these Flower-Pickers, whom we caught in the very act of picking your flowers."

"Shameful!" the queen said. "And criminal! Picking my beautiful flowers is strictly against the Law of the Stingerbugs!"

Poppy stepped forward, grabbed the bars of the cage, and stuck her head through. "Your Majesty, we didn't know anything about your law. We only wanted to—"

"Ignorance is no excuse!" the queen interrupted. "And how dare you address me directly! You are a mere commoner!"

Satin stepped forward. "Poppy just happens

to be OUR queen! The queen of the Trolls!"

The Stingerbugs made a strange buzzing sound—short buzzes with spaces in between. The Trolls realized they were laughing.

"You?" the queen sneered. "A queen? I hardly think so!"

"What are you going to do to us?" Poppy asked.

"Hmm," the queen said, thinking it over. "I'm not sure. Perhaps we shall *eat* you!"

Now it was Karma's turn to laugh. "Eat us? She's bluffing. Stingerbugs only eat nectar and honey. They'd never eat us!"

The queen looked angry. "Perhaps not. But we could sting you. Tell me that Stingerbugs don't sting!"

Poppy turned to Karma. "Do they?" she

whispered. "Do stingerbugs sting?"

"Oh, yes," Karma whispered back, nodding. "But Stingerbugs can't resist a challenge. They never turn one down! Never!"

"Interesting," Poppy whispered.

"What are you Flower-Pickers whispering about?" the queen demanded.

"Oh, nothing, Your Majesty," Poppy said. "It's just that this is the time of day when we Trolls usually challenge whoever we're with to a contest. You wouldn't be interested."

All the Stingerbugs looked intrigued. "What sort of a contest?" the queen asked.

Poppy thought fast. "Let's see . . . what day is it? Oh, yes—well, on this day of the week, we always challenge someone to a contest of . . . strength. But you wouldn't be interested in that. On with our punishment!"

"Just a moment," the queen said. "*I* will decide when it's time for punishment! First, let's have a contest of strength! Buzzer, step forward!"

From the shadows at the back of the chamber, a huge Stingerbug came forward. He was the biggest of all the Stingerbugs.

The queen smiled. "Buzzer shall serve as our champion. Who will compete for the Flower-Pickers?"

"Oh, we don't care," Poppy said casually. "We'll let you pick. But when we win, will you let us go?"

"Certainly," the queen said, sure of her victory. "But you won't win. Because I choose THAT ONE!"

Just as Poppy had anticipated, the queen pointed at Smidge, the smallest of the trapped Trolls.

The Stingerbugs laughed their strange, buzzing laughs again.

"An excellent choice, Your Majesty!" said the big Stingerbug who had captured Poppy. "We are sure to win!"

"Thank you," the queen said. "And now, Buzzer, show these criminals what true strength looks like!"

The huge Stingerbug walked up to the massive throne. "Pardon me," he said in a deep buzz, gesturing for her to move off her throne.

The queen stepped down and stood next to the fallen column. Buzzer lifted the heavy throne over his head, grunting loudly. The Stingerbugs cheered. Buzzer dropped the throne back down to the floor. *WHAM!*

"Your turn," the queen said, sitting on her throne. "What would you like to lift? An acorn, perhaps? We could probably find a nice little one." The Stingerbugs laughed.

"I think I'll try that throne," Smidge said. The Stingerbugs laughed even harder.

"Excellent! This should be good!" the queen said. "Let her out of the cage!"

As the guards opened the cage door, the queen started to get off her throne again.

"Oh, that's all right," Smidge said. "You can stay on it."

The Stingerbugs looked confused. The queen slowly settled back onto her throne.

Smidge walked across the chamber, slipped her hair under the throne . . . and lifted it high in the air with the queen sitting on it!

The Stingerbugs gasped! The Trolls cheered!

"Yeah, Smidge!" said Poppy. "Way to show them!"

Smidge gently set the throne down. "Is this your biggest throne, queenie?" she asked. "The way Buzzer was grunting, I thought it'd be a lot heavier."

The queen was amazed. But she was true to her word. "You've won," she said, "and you may go." She signaled to her guards, who opened the door to the cage again. The Trolls filed out.

Smidge looked at the large column on the floor. "Why is this big thing here?"

"It fell ages ago," the queen said, "and it's

too heavy to lift back into place."

"Really?" Smidge said. "Let's see!"

The tiny Troll slid her hair under one end of the massive column and wrapped it all the way around. She braced her feet and pulled, lifting the column and wedging it between the floor and the ceiling. She gave the column a final tug and it locked into place. *CHONK!*

The Stingerbugs were silent for a moment, too astonished to say anything. Then they broke into loud, buzzy cheers!

The queen jumped off her throne and stared at the column. When she turned to the Trolls, they noticed a tear in her cape.

"Um, Your Majesty," DJ Suki said. "You've got a rip in your royal cape."

The queen twisted around, looking at the tear.

"Yes," she sighed. "That's one of the problems with having a razor-sharp stinger. My cape's been like this for a long time."

"We can take care of that!" Satin and Chenille said. The twins whipped out their handy portable sewing kits and went to work sewing up the tear. In no time at all, the cape looked as good as new.

"Wonderful!" the queen cried. "What a day this has been! I wish I could remember it forever!"

"Perhaps this will help," Poppy said, stepping forward and handing the queen a scrapbook she'd put together in the time it took the twins to fix the cape. "Luckily, I never go anywhere without my scrapbooking materials."

The queen turned the pages, admiring

Poppy's pictures of Smidge lifting the queen, Smidge putting the column back, and the twins repairing the royal cape. "Marvelous!" she cried. "We are in your debt! If there is anything we can do for you, Queen Poppy, please let us know!"

"Well, there *is* one little thing," Poppy said with a smile.

CHAPTER TWELVE

Each of the six Trolls had her own personal Stingerbug to fly her back to Troll Village. On this journey, as ordered by the queen, there would be no falling twigs, or dropping nuts, or rushing streams, or screeching mushrooms, or springy Spring Plants, or greasy Tickle Marshes, or mini tornadoes. And with the swiftly flying Stingerbugs carrying them the whole way, the

Trolls would make it back home in time for the big party!

The Stingerbugs set them down at the edge of the village. "Thanks for the ride!" Satin and Chenille chimed.

"Yes, thank you so much!" Poppy said. "We really appreciate it."

"It was our pleasure," said the Stingerbug who had dive-bombed them in the flower field. "Enjoy your party!"

He started to fly off, but then returned. "I almost forgot. The queen asked me to give this to you." He handed Karma one of the beautiful flowers from the forbidden field.

"Thank you!" she exclaimed. "I love it!" She stuck the flower in her piled-up hair, right between a twig and a leaf. "It's perfect!"

The Stingerbugs flew off, buzzing as they went. The Trolls waved goodbye. Then they turned and ran straight to Maddy's Hair in the Air Salon.

"Look who we found!" Poppy sang as they rushed through the door.

"Karma!" Maddy cried, delighted. She ran to her friend and gave her a big hug. "I was so worried. What happened? Did you get lost?"

Karma shook her head. "Not lost. Taken."

"Taken!" Maddy asked. "By whom?"

"There'll be plenty of time to tell you the whole story later," Poppy promised. "But right now we have a party to get ready for! Can you help us with our hair?"

Maddy shook her head sadly. "Sorry, but there's no time! The party's already started.

Poppy, they're expecting you to light the party torch! DJ Suki, they need you to get the music going! You all have to hurry over to the party right now! Everyone's waiting for you!"

"But," Satin protested, "our hair!"

Maddy pushed them out the door. "Go! Go! Go!"

The six Trolls stood outside the salon. "What are we going to do?" Chenille asked. "Our hair looks terrible!"

They looked at each other. Their hair was greasy from the marsh. It was twisted and matted from the mini tornadoes. It had gotten wet from the stream and the waterfall spray, and then had dried without being combed or brushed. Nuts were lodged in it. And it was still full of twigs!

"I think you look fine!" Karma said brightly.

She thought a Troll could never have too much nature in her hair.

Poppy sighed. "Well, I guess the important thing is that we're here, not what we look like. Let's just go to the party and try to have a good time. I'll light the party torch, DJ Suki will spin some tunes, and everything'll be fine."

She said it, though she didn't really believe it. Poppy was always positive and optimistic, seeing the bright side of things, but even she had her limits. A Troll's hair was very important, and Poppy always wanted hers to look good. Especially at a big party!

Smidge said, "Poppy's right. We found Karma and rescued her from the Stingerbugs. We should go to the party and celebrate, no matter how stupid or crazy our hair looks!"

Poppy stood up straight, threw back her shoulders, and picked a twig out of her hair. "Let's do this!"

She strode off toward the party in the center of Troll Village, followed by her five friends.

ℓℓℓℓℓℓℓℓ

At the party, Trolls milled around. Without the party torch and the music, it didn't really seem like a party.

Biggie looked around anxiously. "Where's Poppy?" he kept asking everyone. "And Smidge? And Satin? And Chenille? And DJ Suki? And Karma?"

"You've already asked me that—like, a hundred times!" Branch complained. He looked splendid with the new hairstyle Maddy had given him. "I keep telling you, I don't know!

But I'm sure Poppy will be here. Why are you so worried?"

"I'm not worried," Biggie lied. "But Mr. Dinkles is." He stroked his pet worm's back reassuringly.

Then Cooper spotted the six Trolls walking toward the party. "Here they come!" he announced, pointing. Everyone turned to look at Poppy and the others.

They walked up with their wild hair, and everyone stared.

"Hi!" Poppy said a little nervously. "Come on! Let's get this party started!"

The other Trolls just stood there, gawking.

"Look at their hair!" Guy Diamond said.

"That's . . . unbelievable!" Harper sputtered.

"UNG GUH MMMNN!" Fuzzbert added.

"It's . . . INCREDIBLE!" Cooper said. "I LOVE IT!"

"It's the new look!" Guy Diamond announced.

Everybody loved their hair! They all crowded around Poppy and her friends, asking how they'd gotten their hair to look like that.

Maddy walked up. She'd finally closed her salon and was ready for the big party.

"Maddy!" Guy Diamond said, running over to her. "Can you make my hair look like theirs? Please?"

"And mine?" "And mine, too?" asked lots of other Trolls, running up to Maddy.

Maddy looked puzzled. "Uh, sure," she said. "I just need some grease, twigs, and nuts."

Just then, Poppy lit the party torch, and DJ

Suki dropped the beat on a pounding dance tune.

"LET'S PARTY!" Poppy yelled, holding the burning torch high in the air. Everyone cheered!

The Trolls partied and danced and laughed long into the night.

ℓℓℓℓℓℓℓℓ

The next day, Maddy's Hair in the Air Salon was crowded with customers. Carrying buckets of grease, twigs, and nuts, Maddy ran from Troll to Troll, giving each of them the new look.

Thanks to Poppy and her friends, the salon had never been busier. And there had never been a more popular hairstyle in Troll Village!

THE END